The Grasshopper And The Ant

개미와 베짱이

직독직해로 읽는 스토리북 ❸

The Grasshopper And The Ant 개미와 베짱이

| 초판 1쇄 **인쇄** | 2014년 2월 25일 |
| 초판 1쇄 **발행** | 2014년 3월   5일 |

편집	더 콜링_김정희
삽화	허재희
디자인	IndigoBlue_김은경
E-Book	BASRAC
녹음	Charm (주)참미디어
성우	Grace Johnson
발행인	조경아
발행처	**랭**귀지**북**스
주소	서울시 마포구 포은로 2나길 31 벨라비스타 208호
전화	070.4123.3640 / 02.406.0047
팩스	02.406.0042
이메일	languagebooks@hanmail.net
홈페이지	www.languagebooks.co.kr
등록번호	101-90-85278
등록일자	2008년 7월 10일
ISBN	979-11-5635-001-9 (18740)
가격	8,000원

© Language Books 2014

직독직해로 읽는 스토리북 ❸

The Grasshopper And The Ant

개미와 베짱이

Language Books

About This Storybook

Story

녹음을 들으며 본문을 잘 읽어 보세요.
원어민의 발음과 억양에 주의하여 따라 해 보세요.

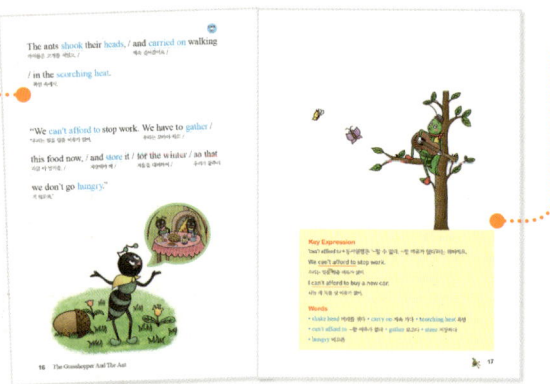

Key Expression & Words

본문 중에 꼭 익혀야 할 주요 표현을 뽑았어요. 그리고 사전 없이 쉽게 읽을 수 있도록 다양한 어휘를 수록했어요.

Mini Test

간단한 문제들을 통해 읽은 내용에 대해 얼마나 이해했는지 확인해 보세요.

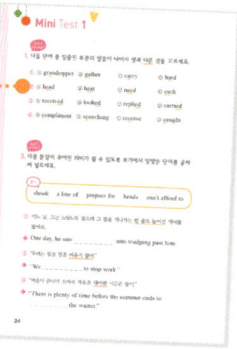

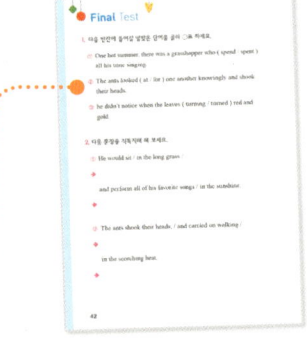

Read the Story in the original

직독직해로 읽은 내용을 바탕으로 원문으로 다시 읽어 보세요. 해석과 단어 없이 녹음을 들으며 얼마나 이해할 수 있는지 알아보세요.

Final Test

여러 가지 활동을 통해 전체 이야기에 대한 이해력을 높이고 내 실력을 점검해 보세요.

About This E-Book

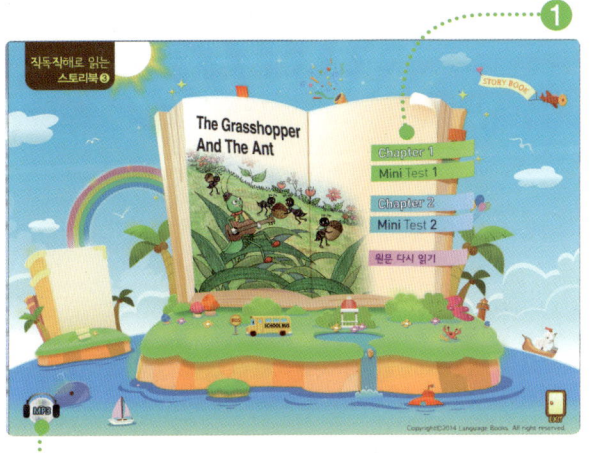

Intro

① 학습하고자 하는
코너를 클릭하세요.

② 녹음 파일만
따로 모아 두었어요.

E-Book Story

③ 해당 코너로
바로 이동할 수 있어요.

④ 녹음 속도를 1~3단계로
조절할 수 있어요.

⑤ 다음 페이지로 넘어가요.

⑥ 모르는 단어는
바로 확인할 수 있어요.

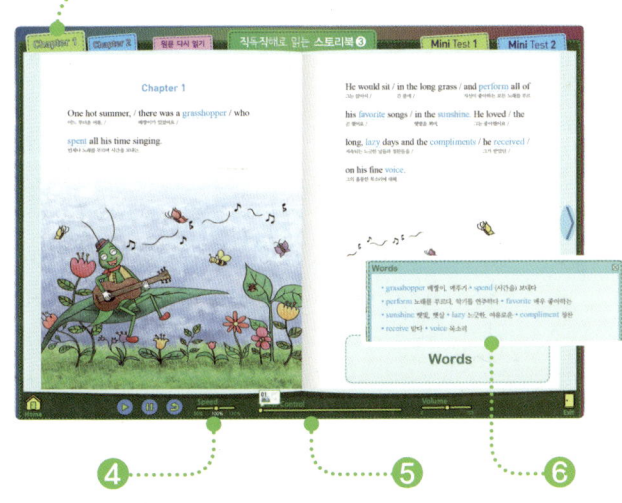

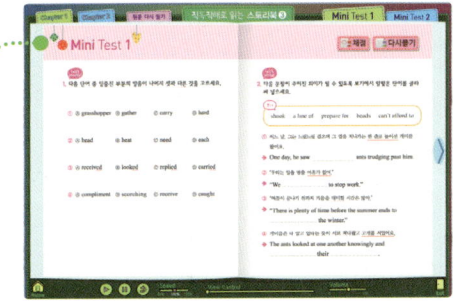

Mini Test

어휘, 듣기, 독해 등 다양한 문제를
직접 풀어 보며 실력을 확인할 수 있어요.

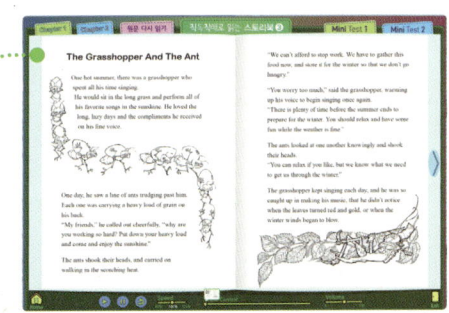

원문 다시 읽기

원어민이 읽어 주는 이야기를
처음부터 끝까지 다시 들을 수 있어요.

About Storybook Handwriting

별매

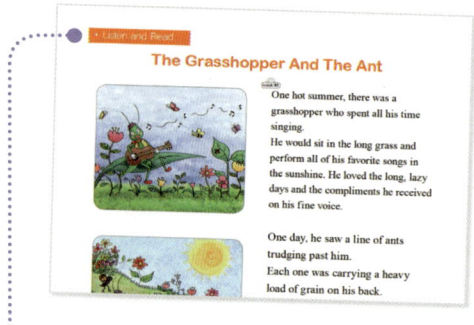

Listen and Read

원어민의 녹음을 들으며
본문을 잘 읽어 보세요.

Listen and Write : the words

이야기에 나오는 기본 단어를
따라 쓰며 익히세요.

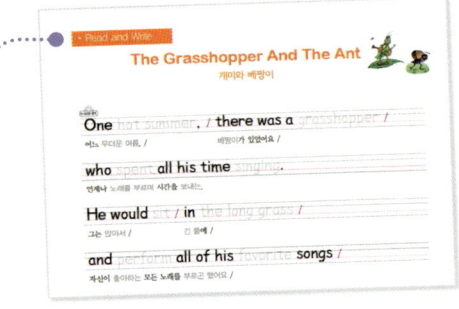

Read and Write

영어 어순대로 문장을 끊어
직독직해 하면서 따라 써 보세요.

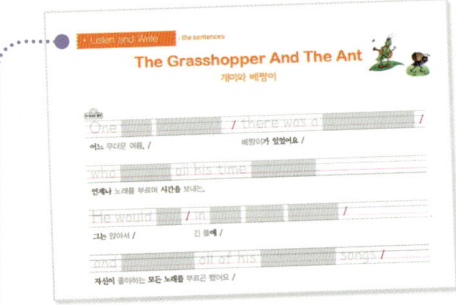

Listen and Write : the sentences

녹음을 들으며 빈칸에
알맞은 단어/구문을 써 넣으세요.

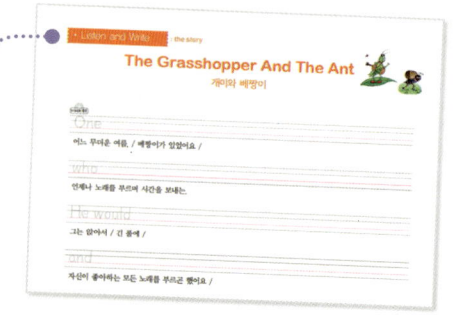

Listen and Write : the story

앞에서 익힌 내용을 바탕으로
영어로 이야기를 만들어 보세요.

Contents

The Grasshopper And The Ant 개미와 베짱이

Chapter 1   12

Mini Test 1   24

Chapter 2   26

Mini Test 2   36

원문 읽기

The Grasshopper And The Ant   38

Final Test   42

Index   46

The Grasshopper And The Ant
개미와 베짱이

* The Ants

천성이 부지런하고 성실하며, 남의 말에 잘 흔들리지 않는 소신을 갖고 있다.
추운 겨울에 대비하여 무더운 여름에도 쉬지 않고 열심히 일을 하는데…….

* **The Grasshopper**

자신의 멋진 노래 솜씨를 뽐내면서
당장 지금을 즐기는 것이 우선 순위인
낙천주의자이다.
여름 내내 즐겁게 노래만 부르며
더운 날씨에 고생하는 개미들을 놀리다가,
추운 겨울을 맞이하는데……

개미와
베짱이

The Grasshopper
And The Ant

track
01

Chapter 1

One hot summer, / there was a grasshopper / who
어느 무더운 여름, / 베짱이가 있었어요 /

spent all his time singing.
언제나 노래를 부르며 시간을 보내는.

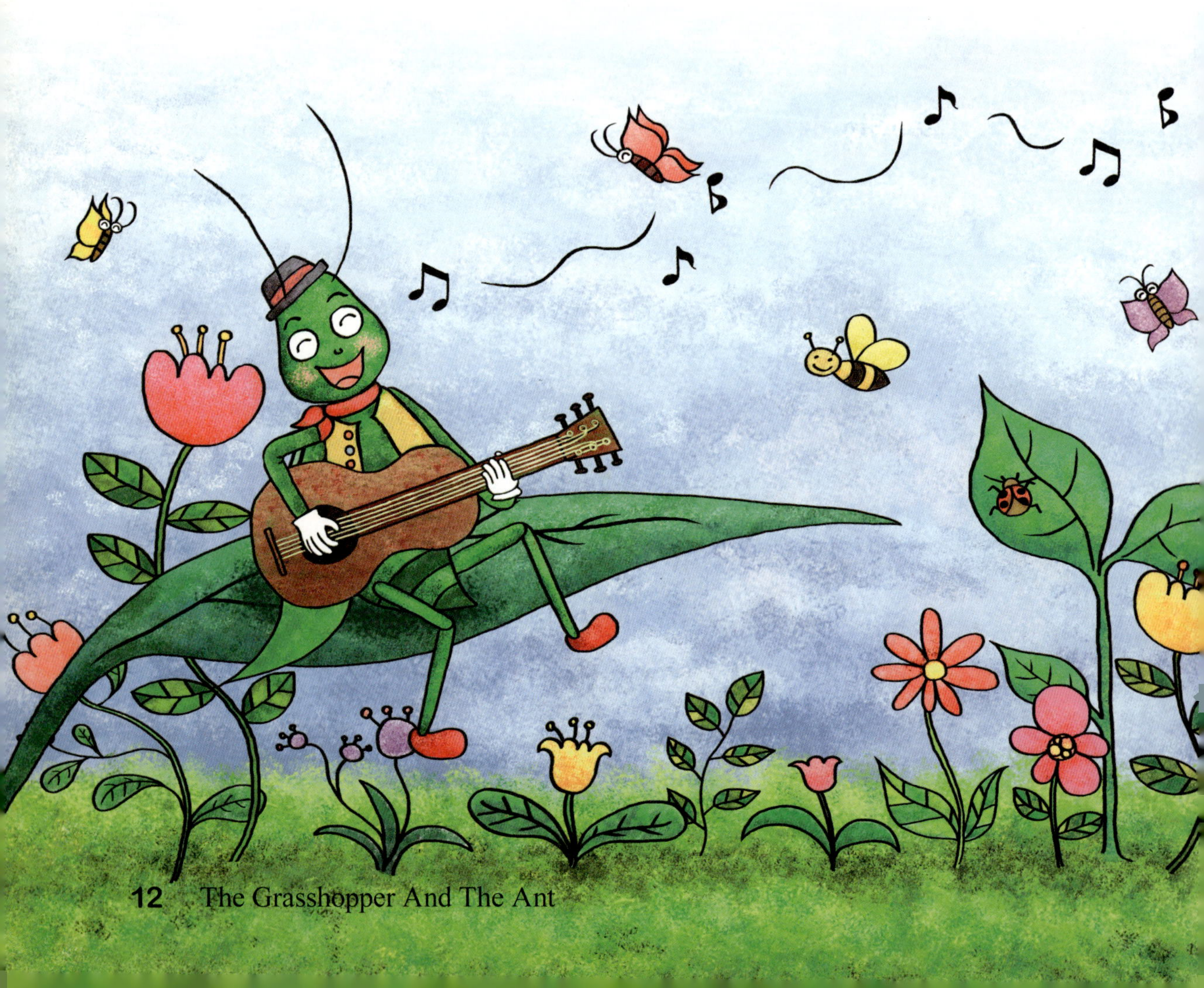

He would sit / in the long grass / and perform all of
그는 앉아서 /　　　　긴 풀에 /　　　　자신이 좋아하는 모든 노래를 부르

his favorite songs / in the sunshine. He loved / the
곤 했어요 /　　　　햇볕을 쬐며.　　　그는 좋아했어요 /

long, lazy days and the compliments / he received /
지속되는 느긋한 날들과 칭찬들을 /　　　　그가 받았던 /

on his fine voice.
그의 훌륭한 목소리에 대해.

Words

- grasshopper 베짱이, 메뚜기 • spend (시간을) 보내다
- perform 노래를 부르다, 악기를 연주하다 • favorite 매우 좋아하는
- sunshine 햇빛, 햇살 • lazy 느긋한, 여유로운 • compliment 칭찬
- receive 받다 • voice 목소리

track 02

One day, / he saw a line of ants / trudging past him.
어느 날, / 그는 한 줄로 늘어선 개미를 봤어요 / 느릿느릿 걸으며 그 옆을 지나가는.

Each one was carrying / a heavy load of grain / on his back.
개미들은 각각 나르고 있었어요 / 한 짐이나 되는 무거운 곡식을 / 등에.

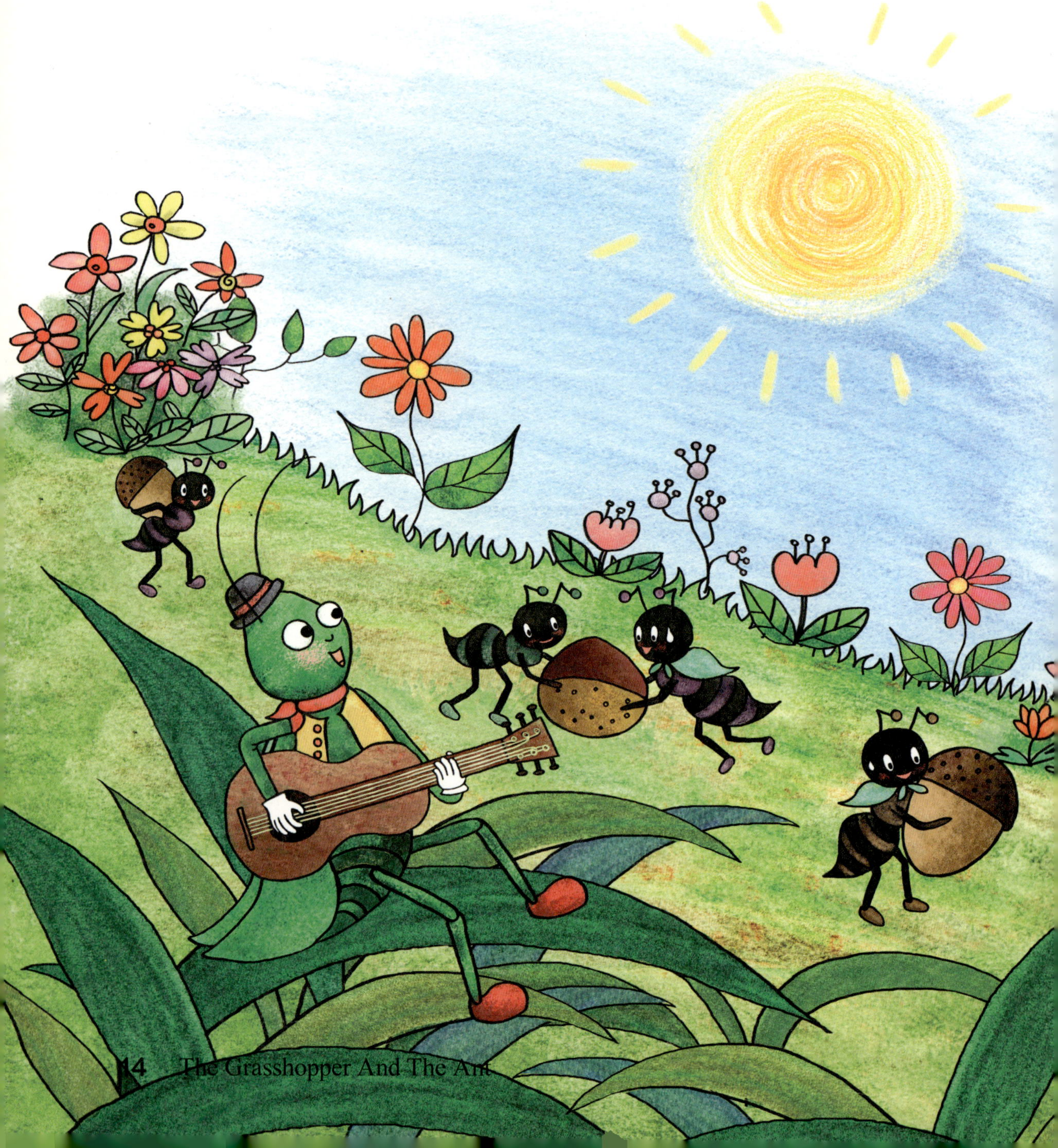

"My friends," / he called out cheerfully, / "why are
"친구들이여," /   그는 즐겁게 소리쳤어요, /   "왜 너희들은 일하

you working / so hard? Put down your heavy load /
고 있니 /   그렇게 열심히? 너희들의 무거운 짐을 내려놓고 /

and come and enjoy the sunshine."
와서 햇볕을 즐기자."

Words

- a line of 한 줄로 늘어선 • trudge (무거운 것을 들고) 느릿느릿 걷다
- carry 나르다 • heavy 무거운 • load 짐 • grain 곡물 • cheerfully 즐겁게
- hard 힘들게 • put down 내려놓다 • enjoy 즐기다

The ants shook their heads, / and carried on walking
개미들은 고개를 저었고, /   계속 걸어갔어요 /

/ in the scorching heat.
폭염 속에서.

"We can't afford to stop work. We have to gathcr /
"우리는 일을 멈출 여유가 없어.   우리는 모아야 하고 /

this food now, / and store it / for the winter / so that
지금 이 양식을, /   저장해야 해 /   겨울을 대비하여 /   우리가 굶주리

we don't go hungry."
지 않도록."

Key Expression

'can't afford to＋동사원형'은 '~할 수 없다, ~할 여유가 없다'라는 의미예요.

We can't afford to stop work.

우리는 일을 멈출 여유가 없어.

I can't afford to buy a new car.

나는 새 차를 살 여유가 없어.

Words

- shake head 머리를 젓다 • carry on 계속 가다 • scorching heat 폭염
- can't afford to ~할 여유가 없다 • gather 모으다 • store 저장하다
- hungry 배고픈

"You worry too much," / said the grasshopper, /
"너희들은 너무 많이 걱정하는구나," / 베짱이는 말했고, /

warming up his voice / to begin singing / once
목을 천천히 풀었어요 / 노래를 시작하기 위해 / 또 다시.

again.

"There is plenty of time / before the summer ends /
"시간은 많아 /   여름이 끝나기 전까지 /

to prepare for the winter. You should relax and have
겨울을 대비할.   쉬며 재미있게 놀아야지 /

some fun / while the weather is fine."
            날씨가 좋은 동안에는."

track 05

The ants looked at one another / knowingly / and
개미들은 서로 쳐다봤고 / 다 알고 있다는 듯이 /

shook their heads.
고개를 저었어요.

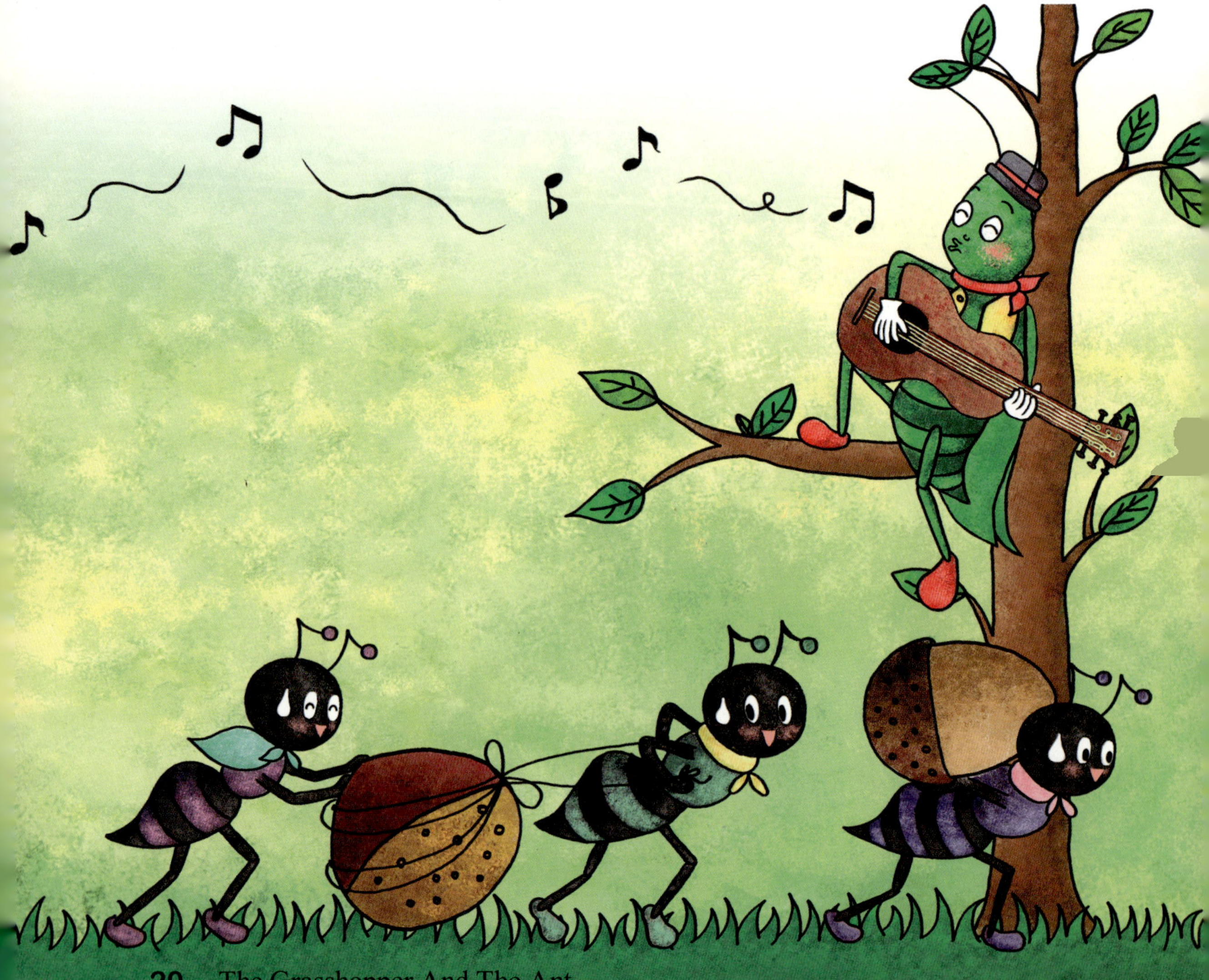

"You can relax / if you like, / but we know / what
"쉴 수 있지 /   네가 원하면, /   하지만 우리는 알아 /   무엇이 필요한

we need / to get us through the winter."
지 /   겨울을 쭉 지내려면."

Words

• look at ~을 보다 • one another 서로 • knowingly 다 알고 있듯이

• through 어떤 시기의 처음부터 끝까지

track 06

The grasshopper kept singing each day, / and he
베짱이는 날마다 계속 노래를 불렀고, /

was so caught up / in making his music, / that he
그는 매우 열중해서 / 노래를 부르는 일에, / 알아차리지 못했어

didn't notice / when the leaves turned red and gold,
요 / 언제 나뭇잎들이 붉은 색과 금색으로 변했는지, /

/ or when the winter winds began to blow.
또는 언제 겨울 바람이 불기 시작했는지.

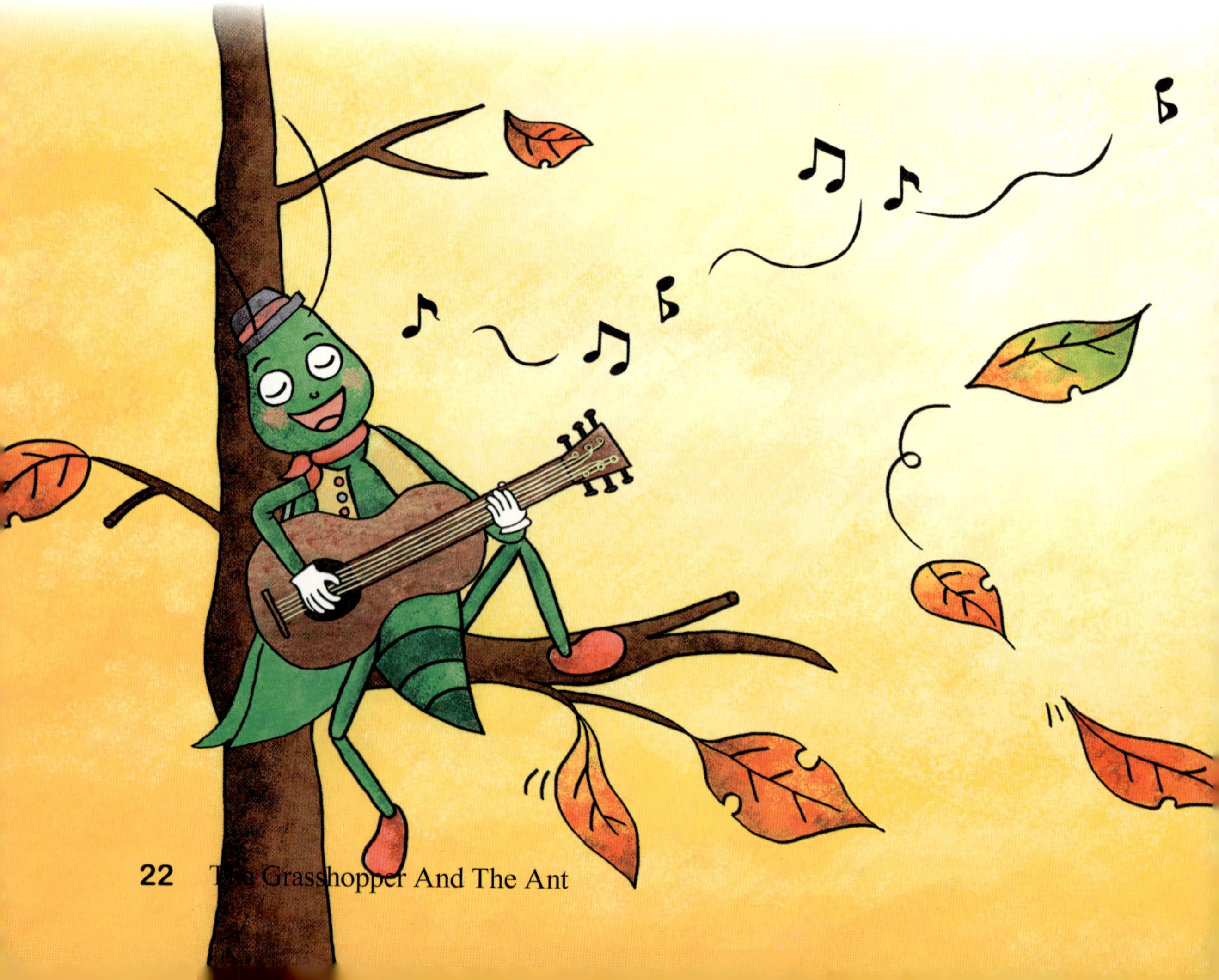

Key Expression

'keep+동사+-ing'는, '계속 ~하다'라는 의미예요.

The grasshopper <u>kept singing</u> / each day.

베짱이는 계속 노래를 불렀어요 / 날마다.

My car <u>kept breaking</u> down.

내 차는 계속 고장 났어.

Words

• each day 날마다 • caught up in ~에 휘말려 들다 • notice 알아차리다

• turn ~로 되다, 변하다 • blow 불다

Mini Test 1

Let's choose!

1. 다음 단어 중 밑줄친 부분의 발음이 나머지 셋과 <u>다른</u> 것을 고르세요.

① ⒜ g<u>ra</u>sshopper ⒝ g<u>a</u>ther ⒞ c<u>a</u>rry ⒟ h<u>a</u>rd

② ⒜ h<u>ea</u>d ⒝ h<u>ea</u>t ⒞ n<u>ee</u>d ⒟ <u>ea</u>ch

③ ⒜ receiv<u>ed</u> ⒝ look<u>ed</u> ⒞ repli<u>ed</u> ⒟ carri<u>ed</u>

④ ⒜ <u>c</u>ompliment ⒝ <u>sc</u>orching ⒞ re<u>c</u>eive ⒟ <u>c</u>aught

Let's write!

2. 다음 문장이 주어진 의미가 될 수 있도록 보기에서 알맞은 단어를 골라 써 넣으세요.

보기

shook   a line of   prepare for   heads   can't afford to

① 어느 날, 그는 느릿느릿 걸으며 그 옆을 지나가는 <u>한 줄로 늘어선</u> 개미를 봤어요.

➡ One day, he saw ＿＿＿＿＿＿ ants trudging past him.

② "우리는 일을 멈출 <u>여유가 없어</u>."

➡ "We ＿＿＿＿＿＿ to stop work."

③ "여름이 끝나기 전까지 겨울을 <u>대비할</u> 시간은 많아."

➡ "There is plenty of time before the summer ends to ＿＿＿＿＿＿ the winter."

24

④ 개미들은 다 알고 있다는 듯이 서로 쳐다봤고 <u>고개를 저었어요</u>.

➡ The ants looked at one another knowingly and

_____ their _____.

3. 다음 녹음을 듣고, 보기에서 빈칸에 알맞은 단어를 골라 써 넣으세요.

> 보기
>
> heavy   once again   caught up in   compliments

① He loved the long, lazy days and the _____ he received on his fine voice.

② Each one was carrying a _____ load of grain on his back.

③ "You worry too much," said the grasshopper, warming up his voice to begin singing _____.

④ The grasshopper kept singing each day, and he was so _____ making his music, that he didn't notice when the leaves turned red and gold, or when the winter winds began to blow.

Answer 1. ①—ⓓ / ②—ⓐ / ③—ⓑ / ④—ⓒ
2. ① a line of ② can't afford to ③ prepare for ④ shook / heads
3. ① compliments ② heavy ③ once again ④ caught up in

track 07

Chapter 2

Before too long, / the poor grasshopper was
곧, / 가련한 베짱이는 떨고 있었고 /

shivering / with cold, / and starving hungry.
추위로, / 배고픔에 굶주렸어요.

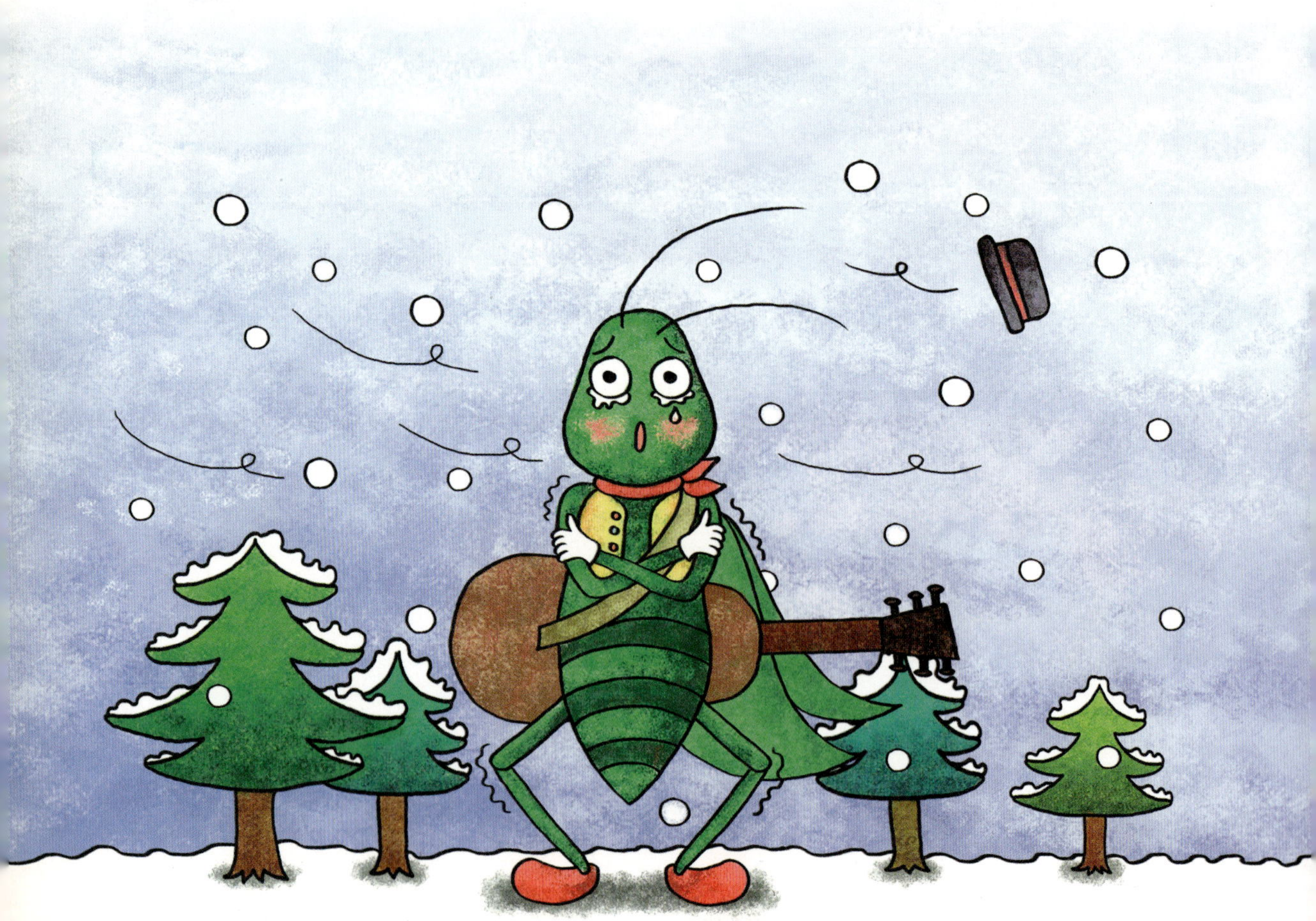

As the snow began to fall, / he could find nothing at

눈이 내리기 시작했기 때문에, / 그는 먹을 것을 전혀 찾을 수 없었어요, /

all to eat, / though he searched / as hard as he could

비록 그가 찾았지만 / 가능한 한 열심히 /

/ in the frosty grass.

서리가 내린 풀 속에서.

Words

• shiver (몸을) 떨다 • starve 굶주리다 • at all 조금도 (~아니다) • search 찾다

• frosty 서리가 내리는

track 08

His search took him / to the door of the ants' house,
먹을 것을 찾다보니 / 개미네 집의 문까지 갔는데, /

/ which looked warm and cosy.
따뜻하고 아늑해 보였어요.

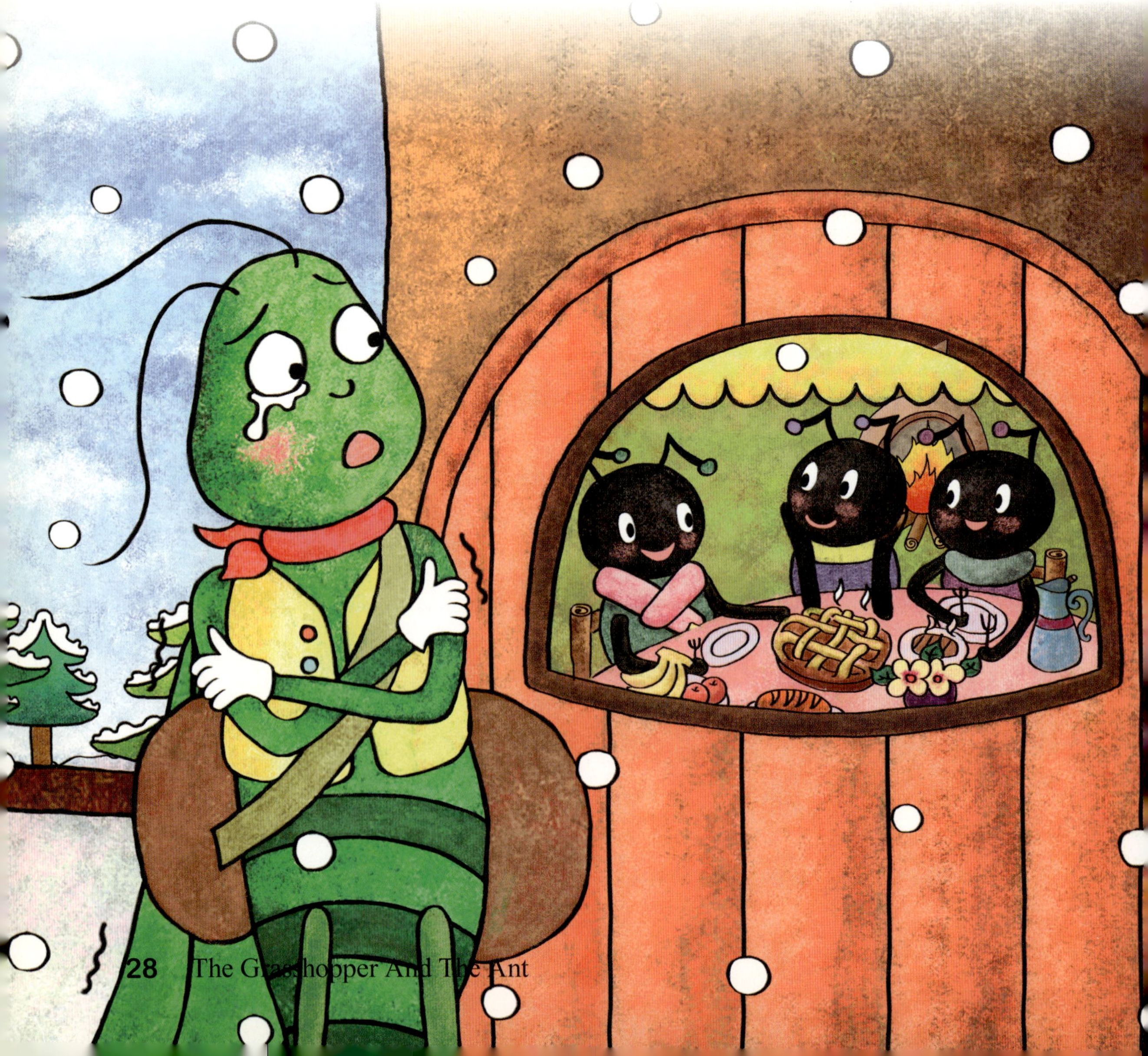

When he looked / through the window, / he could
그가 보았을 때 /   창문으로, /   그는 볼 수 있었어요 /

see / the ants sitting around a table / and eating a
개미들이 식탁에 둘러앉아서 /   성대한 저녁 식사를 하고 있는

huge dinner.
것을.

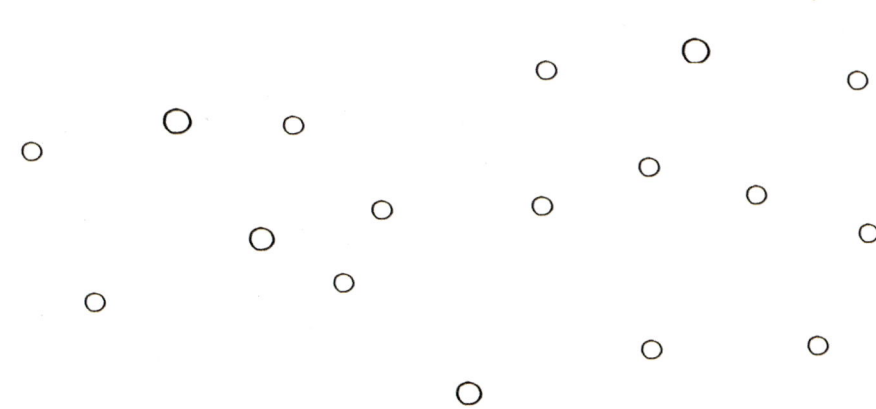

Straight away, / the hungry grasshopper knocked on
지체 없이, / 굶주린 베짱이는 문을 두드렸어요.

the door.

"I am cold and hungry," / he said.
"난 춥고 굶주렸어요," / 그가 말했어요.

"Please may I / come in / and share your food?"
"될까요 / 들어가서 / 당신들의 음식을 함께 먹어도?"

Words

• straight away 지체없이, 즉시 • knock 두드리다 • share 함께 쓰다

One ant looked closely at him.
한 개미가 그를 자세히 쳐다봤어요.

"I recognize you," / he said.
"당신을 알아요" /   그는 말했어요.

"Weren't you the one / who told us / there would be
"당신은 그 자죠 /   우리에게 말했던 /   시간이 많다고 /

plenty of time / to store up food?"
                  식량을 저장할?"

"I was wrong," / said the grasshopper sadly.
"내가 잘못 알고 있었어요," / 베짱이가 슬프게 말했어요.

"I spent all my time / singing, / and now I have
"저는 모든 시간을 낭비했어요 / 노래를 부르는 데, / 이제 아무것도 없어요 /

nothing / to eat."
먹을 만한."

track 11

"Singing all summer, you say," / replied the ant, /
"여름 내내 노래를 불렀잖아요" / 개미가 대답했어요, /

with a twinkle in his eye.
눈을 반짝이며.

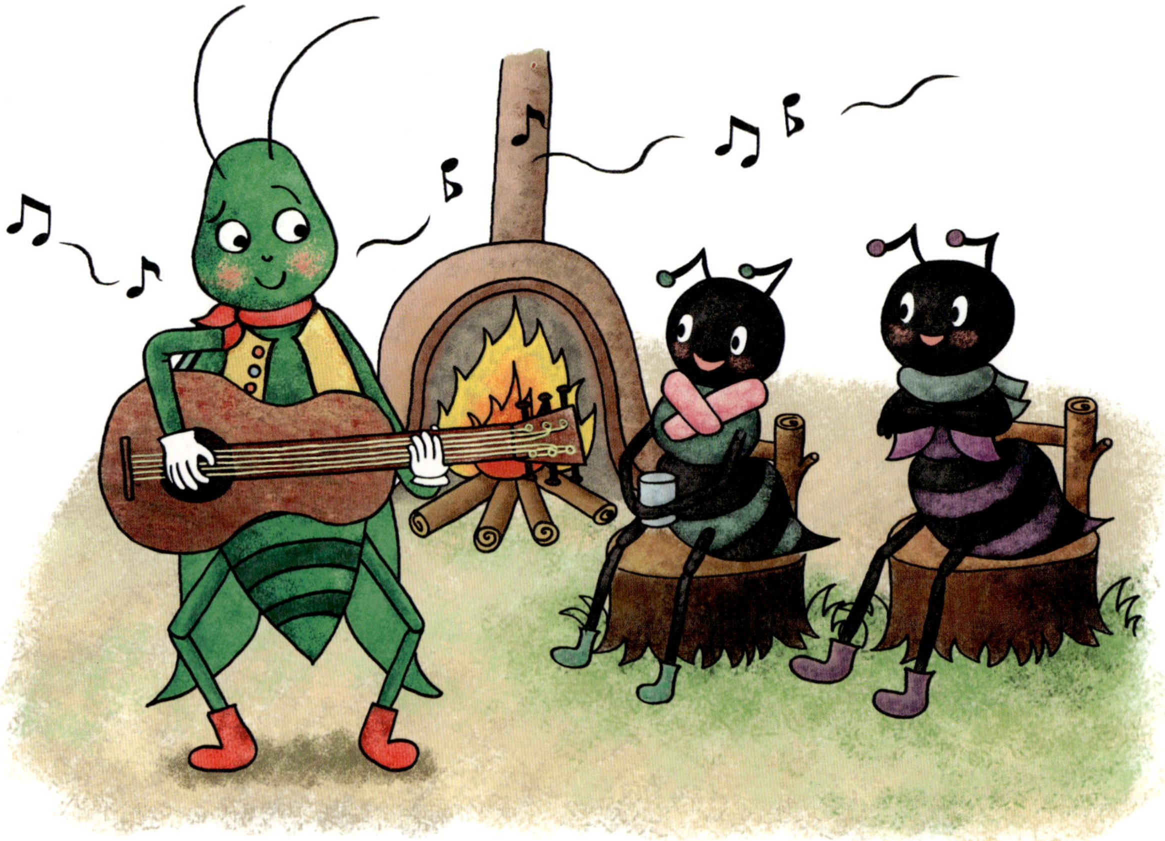

"Well, if you want to share our food / with us / then
"음, 당신이 우리의 음식을 먹고 싶다면 /   우리와 함께 /   그러면

you'll have to sing / for your supper as well."
노래를 불러야 해요 /   저녁 식사를 얻어먹는 대가로"

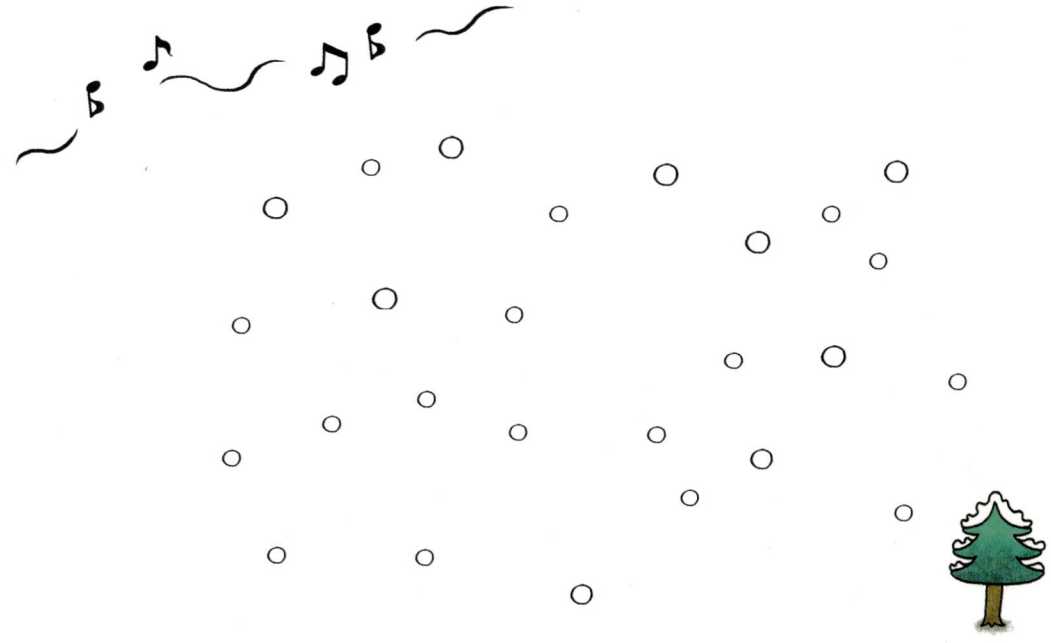

Words

• reply 대답하다 • twinkle 반짝거림 • then 그러면 • supper 저녁 식사

35

Mini Test 2

1. 의미상 서로 어울리는 단어를 찾아 연결해 보세요.

① knock ·   · Ⓐ head

② shake ·   · Ⓑ load

③ perform ·   · Ⓒ door

④ carry ·   · Ⓓ song

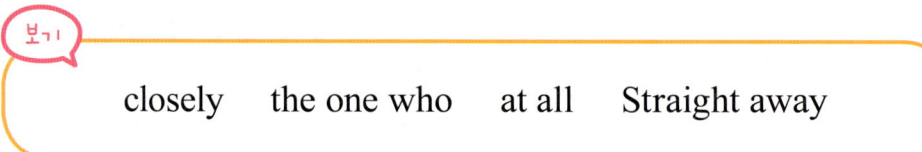

2. 다음 문장이 주어진 의미가 될 수 있도록 보기에서 알맞은 단어를 골라 써 넣으세요.

> **보기**
>
> closely   the one who   at all   Straight away

① 눈이 내리기 시작했기 때문에, 그는 먹을 것을 <u>전혀</u> 찾을 수 없었어요.

➡ As the snow began to fall, he could find nothing
_____ to eat.

② <u>지체 없이</u>, 굶주린 베짱이는 문을 두드렸어요.

➡ _____, the hungry grasshopper knocked on the
door.

③ 한 개미가 그를 <u>자세히</u> 쳐다봤어요.

➡ One ant looked _____ at him.

④ "당신은 식량을 저장할 시간이 많다고 우리에게 말했던 <u>그 자죠?</u>"

➡ "Weren't you _____ told us there would be plenty of time to store up food?"

  track 14

3. 다음 녹음을 듣고, 보기에서 빈칸에 알맞은 단어를 골라 써 넣으세요.

보기

| starving   sitting around   then   cosy |

① Before too long, the poor grasshopper was shivering with cold, and _____ hungry.

② His search took him to the door of the ants' house, which looked warm and _____.

③ When he looked through the window, he could see the ants _____ a table and eating a huge dinner.

④ "Well, if you want to share our food with us _____ you'll have to sing for your supper as well."

 1. ①-ⓒ / ②-ⓐ / ③-ⓓ / ④-ⓑ

2. ① at all ② Straight away ③ closely ④ the one who

3. ① starving ② cozy ③ sitting around ④ then

The Grasshopper And The Ant

One hot summer, there was a grasshopper who spent all his time singing.

He would sit in the long grass and perform all of his favorite songs in the sunshine. He loved the long, lazy days and the compliments he received on his fine voice.

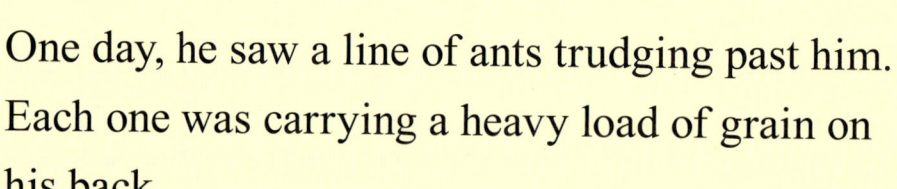

One day, he saw a line of ants trudging past him. Each one was carrying a heavy load of grain on his back.

"My friends," he called out cheerfully, "why are you working so hard? Put down your heavy load and come and enjoy the sunshine."

The ants shook their heads, and carried on walking in the scorching heat.

"We can't afford to stop work. We have to gather this food now, and store it for the winter so that we don't go hungry."

"You worry too much," said the grasshopper, warming up his voice to begin singing once again.
"There is plenty of time before the summer ends to prepare for the winter. You should relax and have some fun while the weather is fine."

The ants looked at one another knowingly and shook their heads.
"You can relax if you like, but we know what we need to get us through the winter."

The grasshopper kept singing each day, and he was so caught up in making his music, that he didn't notice when the leaves turned red and gold, or when the winter winds began to blow.

Before too long, the poor grasshopper was shivering with cold, and starving hungry.

As the snow began to fall, he could find nothing at all to eat, though he searched as hard as he could in the frosty grass.

His search took him to the door of the ants' house, which looked warm and cosy.

When he looked through the window, he could see the ants sitting around a table and eating a huge dinner.

Straight away, the hungry grasshopper knocked on the door.

"I am cold and hungry," he said.

"Please may I come in and share your food?"

One ant looked closely at him.

"I recognize you," he said.

"Weren't you the one who told us there would be plenty of time to store up food?"

"I was wrong," said the grasshopper sadly.
"I spent all my time singing, and now I have nothing to eat."

"Singing all summer, you say," replied the ant, with a twinkle in his eye.
"Well, if you want to share our food with us then you'll have to sing for your supper as well."

Final Test

1. 다음 빈칸에 들어갈 알맞은 단어를 골라 ◯표 하세요.

① One hot summer, there was a grasshopper who (spend / spent) all his time singing.

② The ants looked (at / for) one another knowingly and shook their heads.

③ he didn't notice when the leaves (turning / turned) red and gold.

2. 다음 문장을 직독직해 해 보세요.

① He would sit / in the long grass /

➡

and perform all of his favorite songs / in the sunshine.

➡

② The ants shook their heads, / and carried on walking /

➡

in the scorching heat.

➡

③ "I spent all my time / singing, / and now I have nothing / to eat."

3. 다음 문장을 영작해 보세요.

① "너희들의 무거운 짐을 내려놓고 / 와서 햇볕을 즐기자."

➡

② "우리는 모아야 하고 / 지금 이 양식을, / 저장해야 해 / 겨울을 대비하여 / 우리가 굶주리지 않도록."

➡

③ "될까요 / 들어가서 / 당신들의 음식을 함께 먹어도?"

➡

Answer
1. ① spent ② at ③ turned
2. ① 그는 앉아서 / 긴 풀에 / 자신이 좋아하는 모든 노래를 부르곤 했어요 / 햇볕을 쬐며.
   ② 개미들은 고개를 저었고 / 계속 걸어갔어요 / 폭염 속에서.
   ③ "저는 모든 시간을 낭비했어요 / 노래를 부르는 데, / 이제 아무것도 없어요 / 먹을 만한."
3. ① "Put down your heavy load / and come and enjoy the sunshine."
   ② "We have to gather / this food now, / and store it / for the winter / so that we don't go hungry."
   ③ "Please may I / come in / and share your food?"

4. 다음 문장이 주어진 의미가 될 수 있도록 빈칸에 알맞은 말을 써 넣어 보세요.

① "친구들이여," 그는 즐겁게 소리쳤어요, "너희들은 왜 그렇게 <u>열심히</u> 일하고 있니?"

➨ "My friends," he called out cheerfully, "why are you working so _____?"

② "너희들은 너무 많이 걱정하는구나," 베짱이는 말했고, 또 다시 노래를 시작하기 위해 목을 천천히 <u>풀었어요.</u>

➨ "You worry too much," said the grasshopper, _____ his voice to begin singing once again.

③ "네가 원하면 쉴 수 있지, 하지만 우리는 겨울을 <u>쭉</u> 지내려면 무엇이 필요한지 알아."

➨ "You can relax if you like, but we know what we need to get us _____ the winter."

5. 다음 문장이 본문의 내용과 맞으면 T, 틀리면 F에 ✔표 하세요.

① The grasshopper was sitting in the long grass and perform all of his favorite songs in the sunshine.　　　　(T / F)

② The grasshopper saw the ants trudging past him, he decided to sing songs for them.　　　　(T / F)

③ In the cold winter, the ants invited the grasshopper and shared their food.　　　　(T / F)

6. 다음 빈칸에 들어갈 알맞은 말을 보기에서 골라 이야기를 완성해 보세요.

> 보기
>
> put down   each day   spent   sunshine   hard
> scorching heat   share   load   carried on   trudging

There was a grasshopper who ① _____ all his time singing in the ② _____ .

One day, he saw a line of ants ③ _____ past him. They were working so ④ _____ in the ⑤ _____ .
The grasshopper wanted to let them ⑥ _____ heavy ⑦ _____ and enjoy the sunshine. But the ants shook their heads, and ⑧ _____ working for the winter.
The grasshopper kept singing ⑨ _____ .

Before too long, the winter was coming and he had no food to eat. His search took him to the door of the ants' house.
The hungry grasshopper knocked on the door and asked the ants to ⑩ _____ some food. The ants let him come in and sing for them.

Index

a line of 한 줄로 늘어선

at all 조금도 (~아니다)

begin 시작하다

blow 불다

can't afford to ~할 여유가 없다

carry on 계속 가다

carry 나르다

caught up in ~에 휘말려 들다

cheerfully 즐겁게

closely 접근하여

compliment 칭찬

cosy 아늑한

each day 날마다

enjoy 즐기다

favorite 매우 좋아하는

frosty 서리가 내리는

gather 모으다

grain 곡물

grasshopper 베짱이, 메뚜기

hard 힘들게

heavy 무거운

huge 거대한

hungry 배고픈

knock 두드리다

knowingly 다 알고 있듯이

lazy 느긋한, 여유로운

load 짐

look at ~을 보다

notice 알아차리다

once again 또 다시

one another 서로

perform 노래를 부르다, 악기를 연주하다

plenty 많이

prepare for ~을 준비하다

put down 내려놓다

receive 받다

recognize 알아보다

relax 쉬다, 휴식을 취하다

reply 대답하다

sadly 슬프게

scorching heat 폭염

search 찾다

shake head 머리를 젓다

share 함께 쓰다

shiver (몸을) 떨다

sit around ~에 둘러앉다

spend (시간을) 보내다

starve 굶주리다

store 저장하다

straight away 지체없이, 즉시

sunshine 햇빛, 햇살

supper 저녁 식사

then 그러면

through 어떤 시기의 처음부터 끝까지

trudge (무거운 것을 들고) 느릿느릿 걷다

turn ~로 되다, 변하다

twinkle 반짝거림

voice 목소리

warm up 몸을 천천히 풀다

wrong 잘못된, 틀린